ZOMBIE ™

TROUBLE

THE BIRTHDAY DISASTER

FOR MY SON, ROBBIE, WHO IS
SUCH AN INSPIRATION TO ME,
AND TO SO MANY OTHERS.

Written and illustrated by:

Margaret Montgomery

Chapter 1:

Happy Birthday Robbie!

This is Robbie and his new zombie.

1

He got it for his birthday today.

HAPPY BIRTHDAY ROBBIE

2

Then his mean sister, Jan, threw it in the garbage can...

...and that's when all of the trouble began.

4

Chapter 2:

And so it Begins

There he was at his party, wearing his birthday * HAT...

6

When ZAP!

It was turned

into a birthday

CAT!

9

Robbie was shocked and very surprised. He really just could not believe his eyes!

Had his zombie just come alive and made his words ZOMBIFIED?

What happened next, he could hardly believe!

His bowl of
ICE CREAM was
zapped...

ZAP

13

...into a bowl of

ICE

STEAM!

From there it just got worse and worse.

16

He needed something to quench his thirst.

17

So, Robbie grabbed a bottle of POP...

18

and then... ZAP!

19

He was holding a
bottle of
SLOP!

20

Next, it was time for his birthday song, and he hoped that nothing more would go wrong.

22

He stood there waiting for his chocolate CAKE, when ZAP!

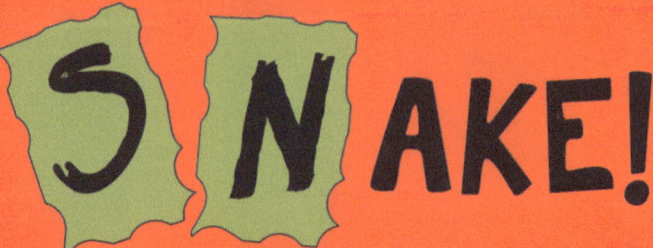

It was suddenly a chocolate

S N AKE!

24

His party was at last all done, and he really wanted to have some fun. So, he went to play with his new DOG, Spot.

Then,
ZIP... ZAP... ZOG

His DOG was zombified into a spotted

FROG!

Chapter 3:

Oh What a Day!

First, his birthday HAT turned into a CAT.

31

Then, his bowl of ice CREAM was nothing but STEAM.

Next, his POP
was ice cold
SLOP.

33

Now, his CAKE is a chocolate SNAKE.

Then, the absolute final straw, his DOG, Spot, was zombified into a spotted FROG!

Chapter 4:

Sweet Dreams

Robbie could not
wait to go to bed,
and get those bad
thoughts
out of
his head.

37

Now, it is finally time to say goodnight. A glass of water should YAWN! make him feel just right.

He turns on the water and grabs a glass.

39

Oh no!

40

Poor Robbie got a big...

SPLASH!

Chapter 5:

Good Morning

All of the sudden he sits up in bed. It was a dream, it all had been in his head!

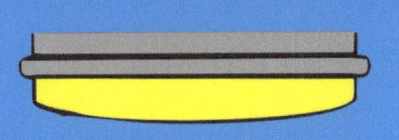

45

He grabs his new zombie and goes out to play. Oh no! It's a YUCKY...

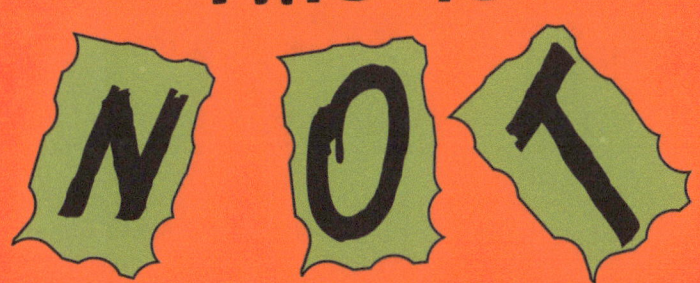

This is **NOT**

The End

ZOMBIFIED WORDS

HAT	⟷	CAT
CREAM	⟷	STEAM
POP	⟷	SLOP
CAKE	⟷	SNAKE
DOG	⟷	FROG
GLASS	⟷	SPLASH
YUCKY	⟷	SUNNY

Margaret is the mom of three boys, and is known as Ms. Margaret in the school district where she has been an aide for nine years. Her youngest son was diagnosed with autism in 2003, and was the inspiration for Zombie Trouble. Her motivation for publishing this book was seeing the excitement that the kids she works with have when reading something fun and engaging.

www.ingramcontent.com/pod-product-compliance
Lightning Source LLC
Chambersburg PA
CBHW041753180626

46815CB00017B/24